THIS WALKER BOOK BELONGS TO:

_____

_____

_____

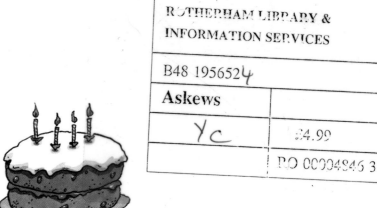

First published 1998 by Walker Books Ltd
87 Vauxhall Walk, London SE11 5HJ

This edition published 2004

2 4 6 8 10 9 7 5 3 1

© 1998 Anita Jeram

The right of Anita Jeram to be identified as author/illustrator
of this work has been asserted by her in accordance
with the Copyright, Designs and Patents Act 1988

The book has been typeset in Columbus

Printed in China

British Library Cataloguing in Publication Data:
a catalogue record for this book is available from the British Library

ISBN 1-84428-460-3

www.walkerbooks.co.uk

Birthday Happy,
Contrary
Mary

Anita Jeram

WALKER BOOKS
AND SUBSIDIARIES
LONDON • BOSTON • SYDNEY • AUCKLAND

Today was Contrary Mary's birthday. "Happy Birthday!" said her mum and dad. "Happy everyday," said Contrary Mary. She loved the presents her mum and dad gave her.

"Much you very thank!"
she said.

Mary tried out
her new stilts – upside
down. Then she piled
her new farm animals into
her new spotty cap and said,
"This box makes
a good hat."

After lunch Mary
helped her mum
make things for
her birthday tea.

She made inside-out

Swiss cheese sandwiches
and iced all the
little fairy cakes
upside down.

Then she went
upstairs to put on
her party clothes.

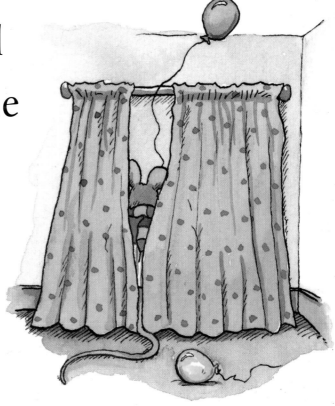

"Come in," Mary's dad said to her friends when they arrived for the party. "We're playing hide-and-seek."

It wasn't hard to find Mary. They played hide-and-seek again and again and Mary was always the one found first.

When they played
musical bumps
and everyone
was dancing
to the music,
Contrary Mary sat
on the floor.

Then, when the music stopped
and everyone
flopped to the floor,
Contrary Mary
danced.

At teatime, everyone loved
the inside-out sandwiches
and got icing on their chins
eating the fairy cakes.
Contrary Mary ate
her jelly with a
knife and fork
and everyone
copied her.

Mary's mum brought out
her birthday cake.
"*Happy Birthday to you!*"
everyone sang.
But Contrary Mary
did not look
happy,
not
one
bit.

Then Contrary Mary's
dad had an idea.

He sang:

"You to birthday, happy
You to birthday, happy
Mary Contrary, birthday happy
You to birthday, happy!"

Contrary Mary laughed
and blew out her candles
and everyone shouted,

"Birthday Happy,
Contrary Mary!"

WALKER BOOKS is the world's leading
independent publisher of children's books.
Working with the best authors and illustrators
we create books for all ages, from babies
to teenagers – books your child will
grow up with and always remember. So…

FOR THE BEST CHILDREN'S BOOKS,
LOOK FOR THE BEAR